D0312199

ELISE GRAVEL

OLGA

WE'RE OUT OF HERE!

HARPER

An Imprint of HarperCollinsPublishers

ALSO BY ELISE GRAVEL

Olga and the Smelly Thing from Nowhere
The Cranky Ballerina
I Want a Monster!

ISBN 978-0-06-235129-6

Typography by Elise Gravel, Dana Fritts, and Andrea Vandergrift
17 18 19 20 21 SCP 10 9 8 7 6 5 4 3 2 1
❖
First Edition

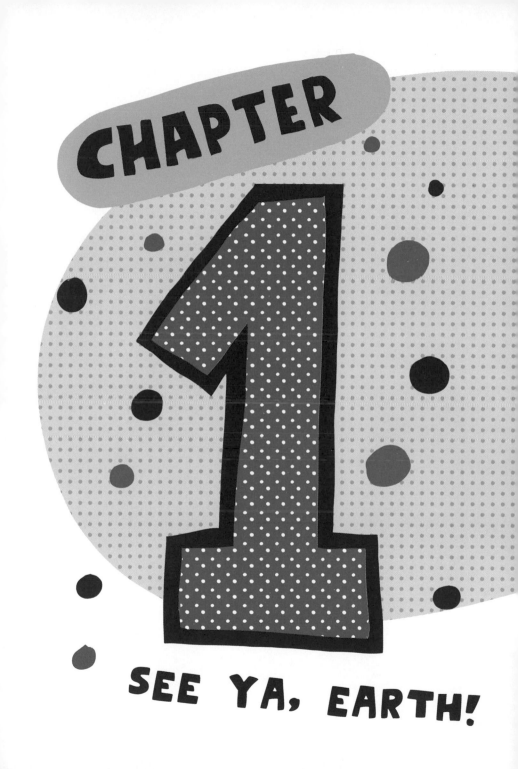

I've been thinking about moving to another planet. I'm half serious about it, too. I know it sounds kind of silly, and probably impossible. But I'd like to hop on the next spacecraft and leave this place.

It's not that I don't like Earth. I like it a lot! (I've only lived here all my life.) There are so many things I like about Earth, like for instance:

THE OCEANS

SUSHI

MY UKULELE

MAC AND CHEESE WITH PICKLES

CHOCOLATE AND CANDY

AIR
(I DO LIKE
TO BREATHE)

COMIC BOOKS

WATER
(ALSO KNOWN
AS H₂O)

BABIES

4

And so many things I would miss!

The list could go on and on. I can't believe I didn't mention bubble bath, gel pens, beetles, movie nights, Play-Doh, hot baths, computers, microscopes, Halloween, bonfires, and my pajamas!

. . . and my bike. Sorry, bike. I just hate drawing bikes, but I DO love you, bike.

As I said, Earth itself is fine. It's all the humans who live on it that I'd like to avoid.

Humans are EVERYWHERE on Earth, and they can be extremely annoying.

FIG. 1:

COMMON HUMAN

(MALE VERSION. BUT I'M NOT SEXIST; THE FEMALE VERSION IS JUST AS WEIRD.)

RANDOM TUFTS OF **HAIR** HERE AND THERE, FOR NO GOOD REASON

THINK THEY'RE **KINGS OF THE PLANET**

BAD BREATH

I LOVE BEER

RIDICULOUS BELLY BUTTON

UGLY TOES AND SMELLY FEET

TENDENCY TO THROW TRASH EVERYWHERE

I MEAN, EWW, RIGHT?

Look, I know that humans do a lot of great things, such as music, or comic books, or pasta. But really, what they do a lot more is fight and destroy the planet.

OTHER THINGS HUMANS DO

THAT I DON'T LIKE:

STEP ON **BUGS** FOR **FUN**

"FORGET" TO PICK UP THEIR DOG'S POO

MAKE FUN OF PEOPLE WITH **DIFFERENT** BODY SHAPES OR SKIN COLOR

STAND **TOO CLOSE** TO ME, OR EVEN **WORSE**, PAT MY HEAD

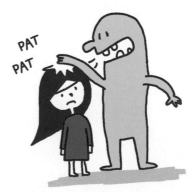

Not ALL of them are annoying, of course. Some are nice, like:

MY FRIEND CHUCK

MS. SWOOP, THE LIBRARIAN

Both are caring and helpful people who I can't imagine would ever throw their garbage in the woods. And I am nice too, even though I'm a human being as far as I know (but I might also be a robot built and programmed by a mad scientist).

I WILL NAME YOU OLGA.

But I've had enough of the rest of them, especially since I met my very best friend forever. . . .

Meh is this extremely awesome creature I discovered a month ago in my trash can. She's round and pink and soft and smelly and utterly ADORABLE.

I did lots of research, but I couldn't find the name of the species she belonged to, so I figured that I had discovered a new animal. Not many new animal species are discovered nowadays except for bugs and microbes, so it was a pretty big deal for a young scientist like me.

I decided to name the species

OLGAMUS RIDICULUS,

after myself, and I think it sounds terrific.

Meh is the best thing that's ever happened to me!

I won't describe Meh too much here because I already spent a whole other notebook studying her, but here's a quick summary:

RANDOM INFORMATION ABOUT MEH:

She sleeps in a trash can.

She's cuddly.

She only eats olives.

She says "meh" all the time, except when she's excited—
then she says:

Up close, she looks super scary, like Jaws.

She's easy to draw from all sides: up, down, front, side.

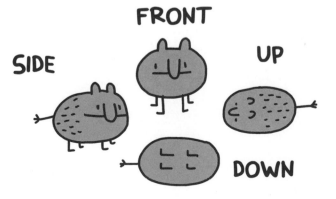

And here are new things I've figured out about her since then:

Meh is so special (and weird) that I'm pretty sure she comes from another planet. Since there are no other known Olgamus specimens on Earth, I wonder: Where do her parents come from?

She *could* be a mix of two existing Earth creatures, like a pig and a capybara*, but I seriously doubt it.

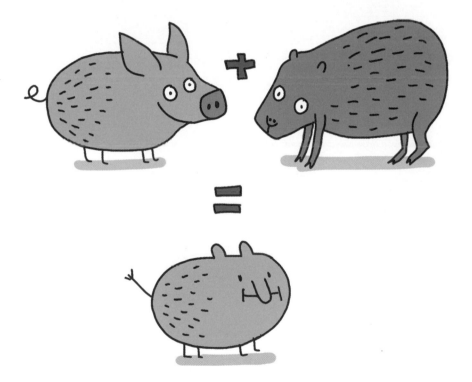

*CAPYBARA: GIANT GUINEA-PIG-LIKE RODENT FROM SOUTH AMERICA.

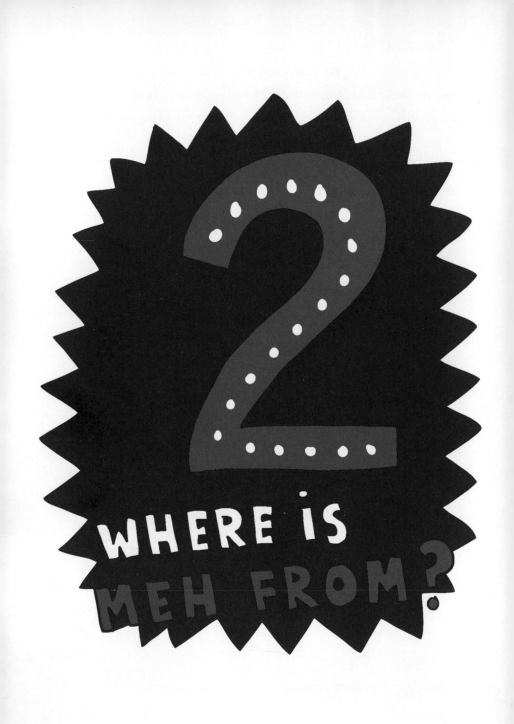

2

WHERE IS
MEH FROM?

Meh is way too peculiar to be from Earth. My alien theory is the only one I like best.

I HAVE AN IDEA!

Meh and I will move to another planet. I can take her back where she came from, and then I'll stay there and keep her company forever. I will get to meet her family, her friends, and her tribe if she has one. That would be

AWESOME.

Can you imagine a planet without any humans, just Olgamuses?

I can. It would be THE BEST PLANET EVER. Although a bit smelly, if I am judging by the only Olgamus I know.

I would bring a hammock and live there among all the Olgamuses, like Jane Goodall with her chimp friends. I would learn how to communicate with them; I would play them ukulele songs; I would teach them human things.

Here are some of the tricks I would show them:

Like any great biologist, I would bring a notebook to record my findings, of course. I already have a number of research questions that, so far, haven't been answered:

1. DO OLGAMUSES HATCH FROM EGGS?

2. DO THEY HAVE NATURAL ENEMIES OR PREDATORS ON THEIR PLANET?

3. DO THEY HAVE THEIR OWN LANGUAGE? MINE ONLY SAYS "MEH" ALL THE TIME (AND "RUBBER" WHEN SHE BURPS).

4. ARE THEY **AMPHIBIANS?**

5. DO THEY HAVE **SPECIAL SKILLS,**
LIKE SEEING IN THE DARK OR BUILDING NESTS?

6. DO THEY LIVE IN **GROUPS,**
AND DO THEY HAVE A **LEADER?**

It would be fantastic. Of course, I would also explore their planet. I'm sure it's a very awesome and interesting place. Here's how I imagine it:

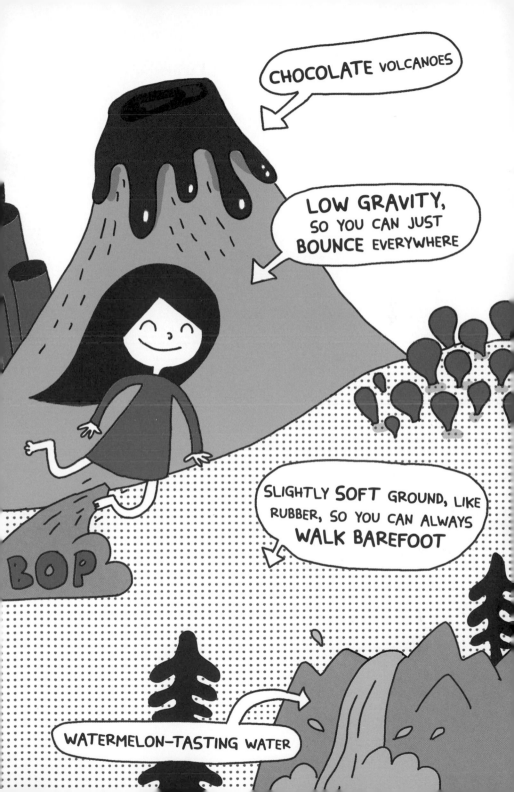

One thing I know for sure: There must be olive trees on Meh's planet, because olives are the only thing she eats. Her planet probably has beautiful olive trees EVERYWHERE! Maybe it looks like Greece, which I found out is totally gorgeous.

GREECE
(IN MY
IMAGINATION)

Of course, if I *did* move to another planet, I'd miss some people from Earth. I would miss my pet spider, Rita, who lives under my sink and speaks French. Or maybe I could bring her with me.

MAKE SURE SPIDERS CAN TRAVEL IN SPACE.

ALSO: DO THEY MAKE SPACE SUITS IN **SPIDER SIZES?**

Would I miss any humans? Perhaps. The one I'd miss the most would be my friend Chuck.

Chuck always hangs out at the dog park. I like the dog park too, so I put away my plans to travel into space, and put a leash on Meh, and we go off to the dog park.

Chuck is there, of course, surrounded by dozens of dogs. I tell him about my plans, hoping he'll want to join us on the trip.

SOUNDS LIKE **FUN**, OLGA, BUT NO THANKS. I AGREE THAT HUMANS ARE **PAINS IN THE BUTT**, BUT I STILL LIKE THEM.

Chuck is good at making human friends. Much better than I am. Even his dog, Mister, the ugliest canine specimen in the whole universe, has lots of friends.

flashback

Chuck and I became friends the day Mister peed on Meh. We all started hanging out after that; Meh and Mister also became great buddies, running around the park like maniacs, smelling each other's behinds and licking each other's faces.

FUNNY-LOOKING CREATURES OF THE WORLD, UNITE!

30

Chuck was right to ask. This idea of mine was probably pure fantasy. It wouldn't be the first time I'd been called a dreamer.

But hey, many scientists before me were thought of as crazy before they changed the world, right?

LiKE:

GALILEO

IN 1610, HE BELIEVED THAT **THE EARTH** WAS ORBITING **AROUND THE SUN.**

LUDWIG BOLTZMANN

IN 1880 HE **TRIED** TO CONVINCE THE WORLD THAT **ATOMS** AND **MOLECULES** EXISTED.

ROBERT GODDARD

IN 1919, HE BELIEVED IT WAS **POSSIBLE** TO SEND A **ROCKET** TO THE **MOON.**

It was time to do what I do best:

The easiest place to find info about space travel would be right here at home on the internet, but I felt like going to the library because I have a human friend there: Ms. Swoop. She's the best librarian ever, and she helped me find Meh about a month ago when I'd lost her, so I like to stop by and say hello from time to time.

Also, I have to admit that I go mostly because I really like to check out comic books. I'm a big comic book fan! Life is not worth living when I don't have good comic books around.

I took a sniff, and it was true: although Meh always smells like a mixture of week-old garbage and eggs, today was worse. I'd gotten used to the smell by now, but I could understand Ms. Swoop's concern.

36

We found a dozen books, and I sat down at my favorite table next to the window.

HERE'S WHAT
I FOUND OUT:

Okay, bad news. Humans HAVE traveled to space, but no human being has made it to another planet. The farthest we've been is to the moon. (Apparently, farther than that is dangerous. Scientists prefer to send probes and robots.)

SOME LUCKY ROBOTS!

SAYONARA!

But they ARE working on it, so all hope's not lost. Science moves quickly. Thirty years ago, nobody knew we would have smartphones by now. Who knows where it could lead us in a couple of years?

I'm still hoping for

TELEPORTATION!

Guess what: A lot of women have been to

SPACE!

VALENTINA TERESHKOVA:
FIRST WOMAN IN SPACE, 1963

SALLY RIDE:
FIRST AMERICAN WOMAN
IN SPACE, 1983

SVETLANA SAVITSKAYA,
FIRST WOMAN TO PERFORM
A SPACEWALK, 1984 (HOW
COOL IS THAT? I WANT TO
PERFORM A SPACEWALK)

MAE JEMISON:
FIRST AFRICAN
AMERICAN WOMAN
IN SPACE, 1993

EILEEN COLLINS:
FIRST WOMAN
SHUTTLE PILOT
AND SHUTTLE
COMMANDER, 1995

OLGA:
FIRST GIRL TO LIVE ON
ANOTHER PLANET

MEH: FIRST OLGAMUS
TO ACCOMPANY A
HUMAN IN SPACE

OBSERVATION #1:

ACCORDING TO THESE BOOKS, PEOPLE DON'T GET TO SPACE BY SITTING AROUND WITH THEIR FINGERS UP THEIR NOSES. THEY NEED TO WORK HARD AT MATH, PHYSICS, AND ASTRONOMY. I'M ON TOP OF IT.

"Any luck?" asked Ms. Swoop.

"Not really," I said. I explained about the limits of space travel.

I thanked Ms. Swoop, took out a few books from the library, put Meh back into my backpack, and went home.

I put Meh to bed in her little trash can, gave her two olives as her bedtime snack, and sat down in my lab. I had some studying to do.

4

THE MUSEUM OF
WEiRD FOODS

Meh's been sleeping for twelve hours and won't wake up. That's lucky, since it gives me more time to study. So far I've discovered some pretty cool stuff about space.

SPACE FACTS:

THERE IS A PLANET MADE **ENTIRELY** OF **DIAMONDS!**

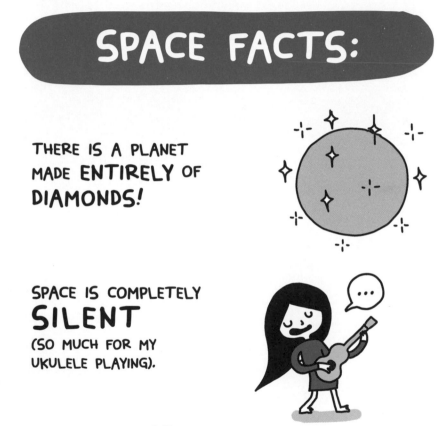

SPACE IS COMPLETELY **SILENT** (SO MUCH FOR MY UKULELE PLAYING).

SATURN HAS **62** MOONS.

PFF!

I HAVE ONLY ONE, BUT IT'S THE BEST.

THERE ARE GIANT POOLS OF **WATER** FLOATING IN SPACE.

IF YOU EVER STEPPED ON THE **MOON,** YOUR FOOTPRINTS WOULD PROBABLY STAY THERE **FOREVER.**

MY FOOTPRINT 4 EVER!

THERE ARE MORE THAN **500,000** PIECES OF **SPACE JUNK** IN THE EARTH'S ORBIT. (HUMANS! DO WE HAVE TO POLLUTE **EVERYTHING?**)

Interesting, huh? After a while, I got hungry, but there was nothing in the fridge.

BRILLIANT SCIENTISTS OFTEN NEGLECT THEIR BASIC HUMAN NEEDS WHILE STUDYING.

I woke up Meh, and we took off to the store.

My favorite place to buy food is the corner store, STUFF 'N' THINGS 'N' MORE!

The owner there, Mr. Hoopah, is another one of my human friends.

FIG. 4: MR. HOOPAH

HOW ARE YOU DOING, FAVORITE LOYAL CUSTOMER?

EXTREMELY WELCOMING AND POLITE

EXTREMELY ELEGANT & HAIRY

EXTREMELY SHINY SHIRT

I told him all about my plans to travel to another planet. He was sad that I wanted to leave but relieved when I told him I can't, because let's face it: I'm one of his best customers.

So I took some time to shop around. STUFF 'N' THINGS 'N' MORE is like a museum of weird products, and I could spend my life in there. Just look at these new finds:

It all probably sounds weird, and you might ask why anybody would want to buy food there in the first place. Well, I can think of

3 REASONS.

Reason #1: I'm a scientific person, and my curious brain makes me want to try out new things.

LET'S EAT **GRASS** AND SEE IF IT'S ANY GOOD!

Reason #2: Mr. Hoopah is an awfully nice man, and truly nice humans are so rare that I feel like showing him my appreciation.

Reason #3: I've actually discovered delicious stuff in his store in the past, like wasabi ice cream or his special homemade popcorn that comes in 99 different flavors.

STUFF 'N' THINGS 'N' MORE doesn't sell only food! It also has everyday stuff for around the house, like:

DANDELION-GROWING KITS

T-REX-SHAPED TOILET CLEANER

TOE EXERCISER

FOR STRONG, THIN AND FIT **TOES!**

CHAMPAGNE-SHAPED MILK BOTTLES FOR **BABIES**

VERY OLD **VIDEO GAMES** THAT NOBODY EVER WANTS

Another thing I like about this store is that Mr. Hoopah always has a treat for Meh and me, like he did today.

"Look, beloved customer," said Mr. Hoopah. "I set these aside for your beautiful pet. They are a very rare, delicious importation from Finland."

Meh is a real olive gourmet, so I took it and thanked Mr. Hoopah. Then he gave me a spaghetti-and-meatball-flavored lollipop, and we said good-bye.

As I left the store, I found myself face-to-face with the Lalas.

For those of you who haven't read my first book, the Lalas are two human specimens who I often find particularly annoying. They've been making fun of me since we were babies, so I would normally put them in the "horrible humans" category. They also kidnapped Meh once and gave her a beauty makeover. However, they did help me with my Olgamus research, so I have since moved them to the "mildly annoying" category.

FIG. 5: THE LALAS

BOTH PAINFULLY **PRETTY**

SMELL LIKE **VANILLA** ALL THE TIME

ALWAYS DRESSED **FASHIONABLY**

OBSESSED WITH POP STARS

BIP BIBOP

ALWAYS WORKING HARD TO BE **CUTE**

ANNOYINGNESS LEVEL TODAY: **MEDIUM**

I still hadn't eaten yet, and

OBSERVATION # 3:

WHEN I'M HUNGRY I CAN BE SUPER GROUCHY, SO I PICKED MEH UP AND LEFT.

I know the Lalas are only trying to be nice, but they always criticize other people's appearance. I call that kind of behavior a "horrible human" habit.

Still, I gave Meh a bath after we ate our breakfast, just in case. I had to admit the smell was getting worse.

SHE LOVES BATHS!!!!

I BATHE HER IN MY **BIG PASTA POT**

HER FAVORITE **BATH TOYS**

While Meh was taking her nap, I had time to think. If Meh came from another planet, there was a good chance there were other creatures out there too. Was I ready to meet them?

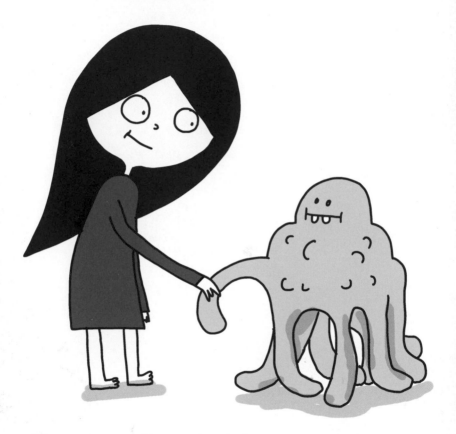

There was nothing about them in my books, so I guessed the internet was going to be my best bet. You won't believe what I found out.

5

ALIEN ENCOUNTERS

If I'm to encounter space creatures other than Olgamuses, I'd like it much better if they were friendly. But do aliens even exist?

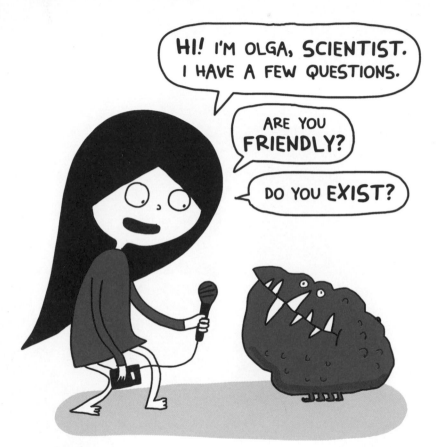

Based on my research, there is no proof that aliens have ever been present on Earth (except for Meh, of course, if she is one). But a lot of humans through the ages have claimed to have had encounters with creatures from space.

Here are some real aliens that people have met on Earth:

THE FLATWOODS MONSTERS: TALL HUMANOID WITH A **SPADE-SHAPED HEAD.**

THE GRAYS: GRAY-SKINNED HUMANOIDS, USUALLY THREE TO FOUR FEET TALL, BALD, WITH BLACK ALMOND-SHAPED EYES, NOSTRILS WITHOUT A NOSE, SLITS FOR MOUTHS, NO EARS AND THREE TO FOUR FINGERS INCLUDING THUMB.

THE HOPKINSVILLE GOBLINS: SMALL, **GREENISH-SILVER** HUMANOIDS.

THE LITTLE GREEN MEN: DIMINUTIVE **GREEN HUMANOIDS**

THE NORDIC ALIENS (OR SPACE BROTHERS): TALL AND BLOND WITH **BLUE EYES.**

OBSERVATION # 4:

NONE OF THEM ARE AS CUTE AS MEH.

This is extremely disappointing. *Humanoid* means "resembling a human being." Seriously, would I waste my time traveling to space if it was only to meet humanlike creatures (who might be ten times more evil than actual humans)?

THE MOST
DISAPPOINTING
ALIENS EVER
ENCOUNTERED

I was hoping to meet interesting beings like

THESE:

I was interrupted from my research by a horrifying noise. It sounded like a defective vacuum cleaner trying to suck up a bathtubful of Jell-O.

I ran to the bedroom, where I found Meh puking all over my best dress. Half-digested olives were spewed everywhere. It was gross.

POOR MEH. YOU'RE NOT FEELING GOOD?

She looked at me with the most miserable eyes you've ever seen. The Lalas were right. She DID look awful.

I went to get the jar of peanut-butter-filled olives, which I found empty. The expiration date hadn't passed—it was just a few weeks away. But I have to say that just the thought of this strange food made me a bit queasy myself. I threw it in the recycling and made a note:

OBSERVATION # 5:

MEH CAN'T DIGEST PEANUT-BUTTER-FILLED OLIVES. MAYBE SHE'S ALLERGIC TO PEANUT BUTTER? INVESTIGATE FURTHER.

I cleaned up Meh's mess, gave her a bath (again), and sat down with her. We cuddled and watched a movie together. That's what I feel like doing when I'm sick, so I figured it would make Meh feel better too.

We watched my favorite movie ever, *E.T.*

E.T. is the story of an alien who gets stranded on Earth when his spaceship leaves without him. A young boy named Elliot befriends him, and E.T becomes a part of the family. But then some really evil scientists want to capture the alien to observe him.

These scientists are so scary! Why can't they just observe creatures gently, like the boy in the movie, or like me? Pfft, humans.

OBSERVATION # 6:

SOME SCIENTISTS CAN BE EVIL. THIS COMES AS A SHOCK.

I WILL **NEVER** STUDY YOU AGAINST YOUR WILL, MEH.

Meh burped softly and fell asleep in my arms. I stayed awake for a long time, stroking her fur, making sure she didn't get sick again.

REAL LOVE IS...

WHEN YOU DON'T CARE ABOUT YOUR BEST FRIEND'S BURPS

6

WHAT ABOUT SPIDERS?

In the morning when I got up, Meh was still asleep. I let her sleep in. When she woke up, I fed her a big bowl of regular olives, no peanut butter. She wolfed it down in her normal way, like a starved seagull, almost choking on every bite.

OBSERVATION #7:

MEH'S NORMAL DIGESTION PROCESS: NO CHEWING, STRAIGHT TO POOP.

I thought that she'd like to take a walk to the dog park, see her friend, Mister, and breathe some fresh air, but when I put a leash on her, she wouldn't move a muscle. (Do Olgamuses have muscles?)

OKAY, MEH, WHAT'S UP? ARE YOU **STILL TIRED?**

I didn't feel like spending the day alone watching Meh sleep, so I called Chuck and asked him if he wanted to come over to my place. Maybe Meh didn't need the company, but I sure did.

Chuck arrived with a bag of homemade marshmallow-and-chocolate cookies that tasted so delicious, it made me reconsider my trip to space.

OBSERVATION #8:

THERE IS NO GUARANTEE

THAT I'LL FIND COOKIES ON ANOTHER PLANET

(SO MIGHT AS WELL STUFF MY FACE NOW).

Chuck and I weren't sick, so we ate the entire bag of cookies in 3 minutes, 53 seconds exactly. They were delicious.

"So," Chuck said. "What's up with your space travel plans?" I explained that it wasn't going to be easy, since traveling to other planets was not yet possible.

I **UNDERSTAND** THAT YOU WANT TO AVOID HUMANS FOR A WHILE. BUT DO YOU **REALLY** HAVE TO TRAVEL TO SPACE TO DO THAT? CAN'T YOU MAYBE MOVE TO THE **JUNGLE** OR THE **NORTH POLE** OR THE **DESERT** OR SOMETHING? OR JUST A CABIN IN THE **WOODS**?

He's right, of course. It *would* be simpler to just go live somewhere on Earth where humans don't go. Jane Goodall lived in the jungle of Tanzania with chimps for many years in order to study them. I could do something like that.

OLGA, THE GIRL WHO LIVED WITH **WOLVES**
(COOLNESS SCORE: 1000)

OLGA, THE GIRL WHO LIVED WITH **SQUIRRELS**
(COOLNESS SCORE: LOWER)

OLGA, THE GIRL WHO LIVED WITH **FROGS**
(COOLNESS SCORE: 0
DISCOMFORT SCORE: 1000)

That's all pretty tempting (well, maybe not the frogs), but I'm not ready to give up the idea of traveling to space. For one thing, I would like to be a pioneer. And also, the whole point is to get to meet Meh's family, or other cool aliens like her.

Chuck understood, although he said that if he traveled to outer space, he would feel lonely out there—even with a pack of Olgamuses. I don't know. I guess I might, too. But there's no way to know until I try, right?

Chuck got up and went to the sink. He said hi to Rita, my spider. He likes her, and I suspect that Rita has a crush on Chuck. She always bats her eight eyes when he talks to her.

BONJOUR, CHÈRE RITA!

BONJOUR, CHER CHUCK.

OBSERVATION #9:

CHUCK'S FRENCH IS WAY BETTER THAN MINE.

"Hey," Chuck said. "What will you do with your spider if you move to another planet?"

I told him that I had to look up if bugs can go in space. Chuck was curious as well, so we looked it up on the internet.

Well, it turns out that many bugs have space traveled! Apparently, NASA likes to send all sorts of living creatures into space. Look at this:

SPACE-TRAVELING BUGS IN HiSTORY:

FRUIT FLIES! IN 2006, NASA SENT 15 FRUIT FLIES INTO ORBIT, AND THE SPACE SHUTTLE CAME BACK TWO WEEKS LATER WITH 3,000 FRUIT FLIES ON BOARD.

SILKWORMS! THEIR EGGS AND LARVAE HAVE TRAVELED IN SPACE FOR DECADES.

ANTS! NASA SENT 800 OF THEM TO THE INTERNATIONAL SPACE STATION TO SEE IF THEIR **BEHAVIOR** WOULD CHANGE IN SPACE.

WE DID IT!

HONEYBEES! NASA SENT 3,500 OF THEM INTO ORBIT IN 1984 AND DISCOVERED THAT THE BEES WERE ABLE TO **BUILD NESTS** IN SPACE **JUST LIKE** THEY DO ON **EARTH!**

SPIDERS! YES, SPIDERS HAVE SUCCESSFULLY TRAVELED IN SPACE. AND GUESS WHAT? THEIR WEBS WERE A BIT **WOBBLY** AT FIRST, BUT THEY LEARNED TO BUILD **GOOD ONES** AFTER A WHILE!

Isn't that great? I rushed to hug Rita, but of course, I can't—it would kill her. So I just blew her a kiss, which made her web wobble.

"Did you hear that, Rita? You can come to space with me and Meh!" Rita seemed totally thrilled. She swung a bit from her thread and smiled.

I was dancing around on the carpet when I stepped on something wet. Mister had peed everywhere, as was his specialty.

"Oops," said Chuck. "Guess Mister needs to go to the park. Wanna come and play some Frisbee?"

7

BAD FRISBEE & SOME WORRIES

After I cleaned up the pee on my rug (YAY! my favorite activity!), I tried to put Meh's leash on and take her to the park. But she still wouldn't budge!

"Come on, Meh! It's a gorgeous day outside. Fresh air will do you good!"

OBSERVATION # 10:

THE BRAKES ON THAT CREATURE ARE PRETTY EFFICIENT.

But no, nothing would convince her. So finally I put her in my backpack and off we went.

Mister was pretty frantic. He LOVES Frisbee. I sat Meh on a park bench so she could watch us. Apparently my Frisbee technique is something special, and Chuck wouldn't stop laughing.

OBSERVATION # 11:

PLAYING FRISBEE
IS HARDER THAN IT SEEMS.

We played for a while, and then we were interrupted by a horrible sound—a cry of disgust.

It was the Lalas. Well, it turned out that Meh had vomited on Farla's shoes.

"Your pet just puked on me!!!"

OBSERVATION # 12:

IF HAVING DIRTY SHOES IS "THE WORST THING EVER," YOUR LIFE IS PRETTY GOOD.

But it was true. Meh was very smelly, even after her bath.

"And what are those disgusting things on her tummy?"

I looked closely at Meh's belly and I saw pink pimples I hadn't noticed. Lots of them. It looked awful.

FIG. 6:

THE WEIRD WELTS

Meh was very sick. I had to take her home. I delicately put her in my backpack and said, "Sorry again about your shoes," to Farla.

Chuck and Mister came with me. We put Meh to sleep in her trash can, and I took her temperature, only to realize that I have no clue what an Olgamus's normal temperature is like, so there was no way to know if she has a fever.

She did feel hot to the touch. I was so scared.

8

ALIEN DISEASES

Chuck stayed with us all evening, helping me take care of poor, sick Meh.

We offered her water, wiped her fur with a wet wash-cloth, covered her with warm blankets, and turned the lights off in my bedroom. I played her one of my best ukulele lullabies, and she drifted off to sleep.

I was the BEST NURSE EVER.

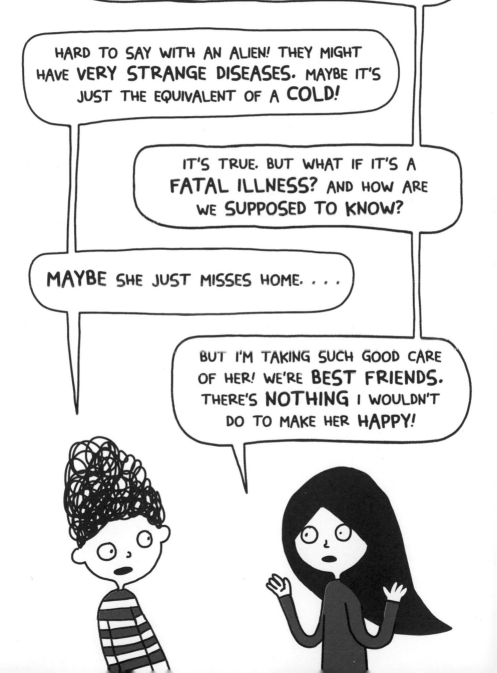

The problem was that we have no idea what diseases affect alien creatures. Maybe they are similar ones to ours, but maybe not.

"Maybe we should go to the library and look up animal diseases," Chuck suggested. "Since Meh looks a bit like a pig, maybe she could have some kind of pig infection."

IT'S TRUE: THEY ARE SIMILAR.

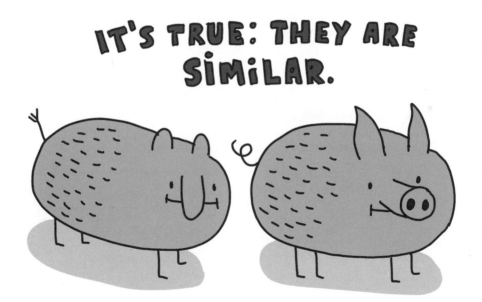

That was a good idea, but I couldn't stand leaving Meh alone in this sad state. Chuck agreed to stay at my place to "babysit" while I went on my errand.

Ms. Swoop wasn't at the library today; instead, it was the horrible Mr. Gumstrap, the other librarian.

So I didn't ask for help. Instead I looked on the computer for books about animal diseases. There weren't any. There were lots of books like this:

Hmmm, yeah. Maybe the adult section would be more help. I love to go there. It's quiet and it makes me feel all grown up.

Unfortunately, there wasn't anything useful to me in that section either. The only book about diseases was this:

I'm pretty certain Meh's not a plant.

I went back home and found Chuck reading comic books on the couch.

I googled "**ALIEN DISEASES.**"

Here are some of the frightening entries that we got:

HUMANITY VS. ALIENS:
THEY COULD WIPE US
OUT WITH DISEASES!

CLICK HERE
FOR HORRIBLE
PHOTOS!

ARE ALIEN SPACE
PARASITES EATING
OUR FLESH?

BACTERIA FROM SPACE
WILL TURN US INTO
MUSHROOMS!

Okay, that's not exactly what I was looking for.

OBSERVATION # 13:

THE INTERNET IS NOT THE BEST PLACE TO
GO IF YOU'RE LOOKING FOR REASSURANCE.

"Hmm," I said.

Maybe a normal vet would do the trick. I looked at Meh, who was snoring in her trash can. If she's still sick tomorrow, I'll take her to the vet.

That night, I put Meh's trash can right next to my bed, where I could keep an eye on her and help if there was a problem. She slept through the night, and in the morning, she seemed better.

She got up, ate a full bowl of olives as usual, and drank some water. She looked a bit bloated and seemed full of gas. Also, her farts smelled terrible, but that's normal for her so I wasn't too worried.

STINK LEVEL:

NORMAL.

I was examining the spots on her tummy, which were still there, when something horrifying happened:

She had never done that before! That's when I knew there was something very, very wrong with my beloved Olgamus.

It hurt. I have to remind you that her fangs are pretty sharp, like a cat's. Now I had two deep holes on the side of my hand, and I felt like crying.

WAS SHE TURNING INTO A WERE-OLGAMUS?

Meh looked at me with annoyed eyes and went back to her trash can. And me? I washed my hand and worried that I might be infected with Meh's disease, so I used plenty of soap and water and a few Band-Aids.

This was extremely worrisome behavior. It was not like her at all. She must have been in a lot of pain to bite the hand that feeds her.

There was no time to lose! I had to go to the vet. But which one? I turned on my computer and did a Google search for "special vet" in my neighborhood.

Here's the page that came up first:

His web page was full of links to articles about him curing famous people's pets and pictures of him at veterinarian galas and conferences and everything. He was apparently the vet to Bip Bibop's turtle, Arsenia.

It was all a bit over the top, but I decided to go with him. Plus, his clinic was just a few blocks away.

I called Chuck, who came to meet me with the carrier he uses when he has to transport Mister.

I didn't want Meh to bite me again, so I used my biggest oven mitts to transfer her into the carrier.

Meh didn't seem to agree with my plans. She started howling.

DOWDOOWDO

Walking to the clinic with the carrier was no easy feat; she was getting HEAVY! And poor Meh howled the whole distance, making people curious.

When we entered, there was a very chic waiting room with tons of pets already. We went to the reception desk, where a young woman named Karen welcomed us.

Karen bent over the counter to peer inside. She had big wide eyes, which opened even wider when Meh started howling again.

OBSERVATION #14:

MEH WEIGHS **40** POUNDS
(WEARING HER CARRIER).

Karen told us to sit down while we waited for Dr. Spiffle to call us. The waiting room was full, and everybody was watching us:

THIS LADY WITH AN EXTREMELY **OBESE CAT**

THIS OLD WOMAN WITH **A SLEEPING SNAKE**

THIS TINY GUY WITH A **GIANT** DOG

THIS VERY
TOUGH-LOOKING PUNK
WITH A CUTE FLUFFY
BUNNY

THIS LITTLE BOY WITH A
BORED GUINEA PIG

THIS ANCIENT MAN WITH A
WEIRD-LOOKING PARROT

Everybody in the room loved animals, just like me,
and after a while I started feeling like these people
were my friends. We talked about our best friends.
We started talking about our pets' feats of brilliance
and funny habits.

Here's what our animal companions could do:

PET FEATS

PUDDING THE DOG
COULD PLAY VIDEO GAMES
WITH HIS **SNOUT** ON
THE TABLET.

$$2 \times 8 = 16$$
$$2 \times 9 = 18$$

SPENCER THE PARROT
HAD **MEMORIZED** ALL THE
MULTIPLICATION TABLES
FROM **ONE** TO **TWELVE.**

COWBOY THE BUNNY
COULD EAT A TEN-INCH-
LONG **CELERY** STICK IN
TWELVE SECONDS.

CRUNCH CRUNCH

VLADIMIR THE CAT
COULD RUN HERSELF A BATH
(SHE WAS ONE OF THE VERY
FEW CATS WHO LOVE BATHS).

BORIS THE GUINEA PIG
COULD **OPEN**
HIS OWN CAGE DOOR.

BERNARD THE SNAKE
HAD NO PARTICULAR
SKILL AND **NEVER** DID
ANYTHING FUNNY.

After about fifty minutes, most animals had been seen by the vet and left. We were next. Meh had fallen asleep in my lap, and Chuck was reading one of the very fascinating magazines that were kept on a glass table. I was getting pretty bored when the door to the office opened. A man came out, holding a folder.

The exam room was bare and cold, with sinister-looking tools, a bright lamp, ads about worms and fleas on the walls, and a row of jars containing liquids and pills.

120

Dr. Spiffle looked more like a movie star than like a vet. His white shirt was unbuttoned, and he was wearing a gold chain. He kept tossing his hair like a horse who's being bothered by buzzing flies.

FIG. 8: DR. SPIFFLE

"So," Dr. Spiffle said. "Karen tells me you have an unknown animal species. Let's take a look."

I didn't like the way Dr. Spiffle was looking at Meh. He looked as if he were trying to figure out if Meh was edible.

"Well," I said, "it's not an UNKNOWN. It's an *Olgamus ridiculus*. I discovered it and studied it and I actually know a lot about her."

"Really? Fascinating! Such a small girl, discovering a species. Heh-heh-heh."

What did he think was funny about a small girl discovering a species? Did all animal discoveries have to be made by tall old men? I was annoyed.

Dr. Spiffle picked up Meh and started turning her this way and that, looking at her from all angles. He probed his fingers in her mouth, which Meh HATES.

As soon as Dr. Spiffle put Meh back on the table, she ran to hide inside her carrier. She was looking at me with sad, pitiful eyes. She looked like:

She didn't like Dr. Spiffle, and to be frank, I didn't like him much either. He didn't take me seriously, and he acted like he knew my own pet better than I did. I felt like grabbing Meh and leaving, but I had to wait and see if he was going to be able to help us.

He took out a notebook and a pen and started asking me questions.

What did that have to do with curing Meh?

He asked a dozen more questions: What did she eat? Did she gain weight recently? Was she aggressive? Did she sleep a lot? What did her poop look like? Did she exercise?

I told him about the symptoms that were worrying me:

THE VOMITING

BLARGH

THE PIMPLES

THE SLEEPINESS

OW!

GNAP!

THE BAD TEMPER
THAT MADE HER BITE ME
FOR THE FIRST TIME

Dr. Spiffle was still taking notes. After a while, he pulled Meh out of her carrier again and looked in her ears and at her behind, and he measured her. This was all new information that I hadn't thought of noting down:

FINDINGS:

MEH IS **20** INCHES LONG

SHE'S **10** INCHES TALL

AND HER WAIST CIRCUMFERENCE IS **30** INCHES.

"Do you think you can help her?" I asked him. "Will she be okay?"

"Well, sweetie, her symptoms are certainly worrisome," said Dr. Spiffle.

Sweetie. I hate that. Did he call his adult male customers SWEETIE? I don't think so.

I didn't like this idea at all. I didn't want to leave Meh alone here with this annoying man.

"Please sign here," he said. "Don't worry. You can trust me, sweetie. I'm the best vet on Earth."

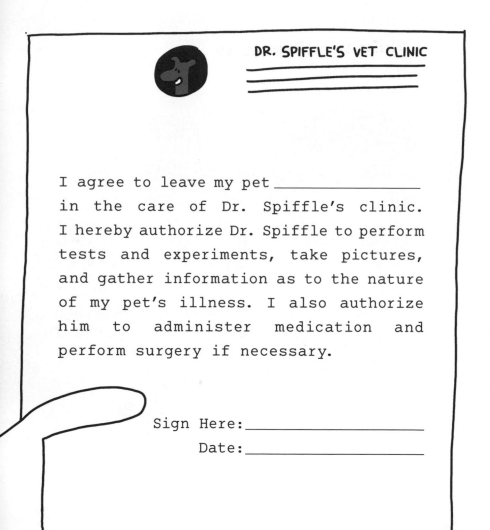

DR. SPIFFLE'S VET CLINIC

I agree to leave my pet _____ in the care of Dr. Spiffle's clinic. I hereby authorize Dr. Spiffle to perform tests and experiments, take pictures, and gather information as to the nature of my pet's illness. I also authorize him to administer medication and perform surgery if necessary.

Sign Here:_____

Date:_____

He gave me a huge, bright, movie-star smile and patted my head. I HATE it when people pat my head. I REALLY didn't like that man.

But what choice did I have? I wanted to do everything I possibly could to cure Meh.

I signed the paper.

I scratched Meh between the ears, in that spot she likes, but Dr. Spiffle took me by the arm and gently pulled me out of the room. She was trembling at the back of her carrier, and my heart was breaking.

And then he pushed me out the door.

Chuck was waiting for me in the waiting room. I must have had a worried expression on my face, because he stood up and gave me a big giant hug.

I was so sorry to leave the vet's office without Meh. Just the way she looked at me as I left the room! Would she ever forgive me?

Chuck took my hand, and we walked out together. "Let's go get a snack at Mr. Hoopah's store," Chuck said. "My treat."

When Mr. Hoopah saw my red eyes, he asked what was wrong. I told him about the vet, and he looked sad.

"I have a surprise for you, dear customer," he said. "Freeze-dried food is astronaut food. For your trip! Come back tomorrow—I ordered freeze-dried olives for your buddy."

Mr. Hoopah also gave us mustard-flavord dog biscuits for Mister. "The treats are on me. I hope our friend gets better soon!"

Mister was waiting for us in the backyard. He was so happy when he saw Chuck that he ran in three-dimensional circles.

I gave Mister a big hug and instantly felt a bit better.

When they left, though, I instantly felt as lonely as if I'd been lost in space, all alone in a bubble. The house was so dark and so quiet without Meh. I missed her snoring and even her weird smell.

I tried to read a bit but I couldn't focus, so I sat on the porch to think. I could see the stars and the moon, and it made my problems seem a tiny bit smaller.

And yet I was still feeling terrible about leaving Meh at the clinic. There was something really strange about this Dr. Spiffle, aside from being arrogant and treating me like a five-year-old. I felt a deep distrust toward this man. His fake smile, the way he rushed me to sign the form and then quickly shoved me out of the room. It all felt wrong.

OH MY GOD!

That's when it dawned on me.

He probably wanted to pretend that he had discovered the new species all by himself! And he looked like the kind of guy who would want his face in all the newspapers!

And what if he was even more evil than that? What if, like in the *E.T.* movie, he wanted to "run some tests" on poor Meh? He had made me sign that sinister paper!

Meh was a gentle, sweet creature! She trusted me, and I'd left her alone in an office with an evil man. I had to go back to the vet's and save her.

I looked at the time. It was 7:42. I had no idea if the clinic was closed yet, but I put my shoes on and ran, still wearing my pajamas. There was no time to lose.

I'M COMING, MEH!

OBSERVATION # 16:

I RUN FASTER IN MY PAJAMAS.
GOOD TO KNOW IF I EVER RUN A MARATHON.

I ran as fast as I could, but when I got to the clinic, the door was locked. All the lights were off except for a room at the back. I heard flickers, camera shutters maybe. I started banging on the door like a maniac.

But nobody came. I kept hearing the sounds of a camera and then I heard Dr. Spiffle's dorky laugh. I stuck my ear to the window and tried to listen. I thought I could hear a faint "dow-dow-dowd," but I couldn't be sure.

There was nothing I could do but wait until the morning. Before I left, I yelled:

Sadly, I walked back to my house and tried to sleep. But it was impossible. I was too stressed out. I had to do something. I had to keep moving. So I decided to pack for my space trip, whenever that happened.

Here's what I put in my backpack:

MR. HOOPAH'S
ASTRONAUT FOOD*
& WATER

A DOZEN
COMIC
BOOKS

MY UKULELE

OLIVES
(FOR MEH)

A PEN

MY PHONE
(FOR THE CAMERA)

*I wish I could leave tomorrow. I can't wait to try the freeze-dried ice cream!

And then at some point, I fell asleep, and I had this dream: I was in this space bubble with Meh, and we were floating over this strange planet, where some creatures were waiting for us. It was

BEAUTIFUL.

. . . And then of course, I woke up, and was back on Earth. A brutal reality. I had to go save my buddy. The clinic opened at nine am, but it was only seven. I decided to leave right away. Waiting at home would be torture.

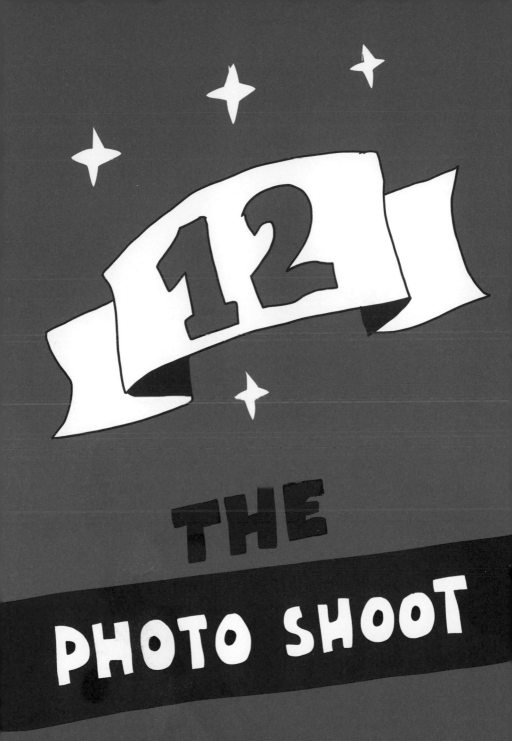

When the clinic opened, I had been waiting on the curb for 45 minutes. A few other clients and their animals were waiting as well.

Karen was at the desk.

I was sorry I shouted at her, but I was very upset.

"I'm sorry, but Dr. Spiffle is running some very important tests on your pet right now. Please calm down. I have strict instructions not to interrupt him while he's working," Karen explained.

This wouldn't do. I was hearing weird noises and laughter coming from Dr. Spiffle's office. I decided to trust my instincts and go in. I took off and ran past Karen's desk toward the doctor's door.

"You can't go in there! Dr. Spiffle is—"

I opened the office door quickly before Karen could stop me. I was prepared for almost anything, but not for this:

Dr. Spiffle was in the middle of a photo shoot.

Dr. Spiffle turned to look at me.

"What's happening in here?" I asked.

"I'm sorry, Doctor," said Karen. "I tried to stop her."

I ran to Meh and took her in my arms. She looked annoyed, but not hurt.

Dr. Spiffle looked a little bit weird. He was chuckling as though the whole thing was just a funny misunderstanding.

"Your Instasnap account?" I said. "What's that?"

Then he took out his phone, opened an app, and showed me a bunch of pictures of himself.

712 LIKES

DR. SPIFFLE ON A BEACH
RUNNING IN THE WAVES

821 LIKES

DR. SPIFFLE ON TOP
OF A MOUNTAIN, HAIR
BLOWING IN THE WIND

612 LIKES

DR. SPIFFLE
ON AN ELEPHANT

DR. SPIFFLE
EATING RAVIOLI

DR. SPIFFLE
DRINKING A LATTE

"I'm a bit of an internet star," he explained. "In my spare time, I like to do some modeling, and I just thought that your, er, pet and I could make some great pictures."

I couldn't believe it. This sounded so unprofessional. At the same time, I was kind of relieved because I thought this guy was plain evil, when actually he just loved attention from strangers.

"Did you even try to cure her?" I asked. "Are you even a real doctor?"

"Oh, yes, yes, yes," he said. "Of course. Please calm down, sweetie. I ran plenty of tests. Here, I'll show you." He picked up a file on his desk and leafed through it.

"Okay," he said. "we can rule out an intestinal obstruction. Her temperature is stable. She doesn't look like she's in any pain, and the welts on her tummy are very possibly some form of acne. One thing I noticed is that her abdomen seems a bit bloated, but that might be due to gas. I wouldn't worry about it. She might be eating too much. I suggest limiting her calorie intake and more exercise."

"Oh," I said. "Uh, thanks, I guess."

"It's been a pleasure. And while we're at it, I made a couple of observations that might be of interest to you. I added them to her file. I'll ask Karen to make a copy for you."

A few moments later, Karen handed me this:

MEH
OLGAMUS RIDICULUS

TOOK BLOOD SAMPLE: OLGAMUS BLOOD IS BRIGHT BLUE.

HER TAIL BONE SEEMS TO BE ELASTIC: BENDABLE AND RETRACTABLE.

SHE HAS FLEAS. (PLEASE ASK AT DESK FOR FLEA SHAMPOO.)

This file was surprisingly helpful. I folded it and placed it in my notebook.

"Thanks," I said again.

"I really am sorry about the photo shoot, dear. To make it up to you, I'd like to give you this visit and a bottle of flea shampoo for free."

I picked Meh up, put her in my backpack, and left.

I guess I was a bit harsh with the doctor. He wasn't really that bad. He just had weird internet hobbies. And I had to admit that Meh looked awfully cute in her unicorn outfit.

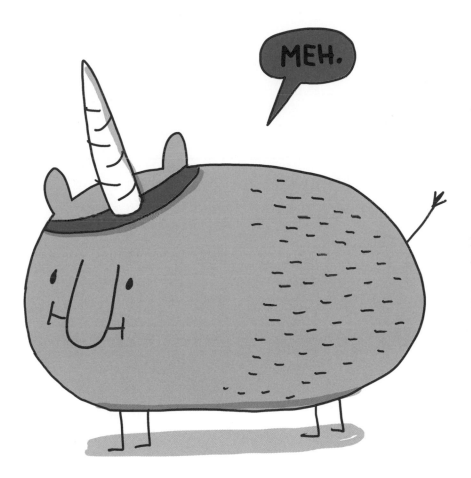

I took Meh home and examined her thoroughly, just in case. She had lost a bit of fur—that might have been caused by stress. She looked exhausted, so I tried to be as soothing as possible while examining her.

OBSERVATION # 17:

PHYSICAL APPEARANCE:
OTHER THAN THE
WEIGHT, NORMAL

APPETITE:
NORMAL TO HIGH

ENERGY LEVEL:
LOW—BUT SHE MIGHT HAVE
BEEN VERY TIRED FROM THE
NIGHT AT THE VET'S

After petting her and hugging her for a while, I sat her up in her garbage can, played her some ukulele songs, and let her sleep. She needed some rest.

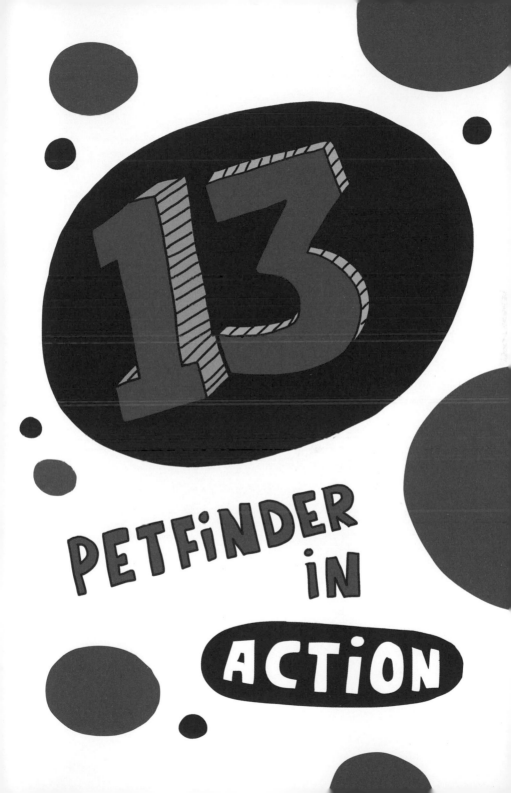

13

PETFINDER in ACTION

When I woke up a couple hours later, she wasn't there anymore.

No answer. I looked in my room, in the bathroom, in the kitchen: no sign of Meh. I looked under the bed, in the closet, under the couch, and in every blanket.

The door to the house was closed and locked, so she couldn't have gotten out.

WHERE WAS SHE HIDING?

The doorbell rang again: it was Chuck.

Meh had a history of vanishing. This time I wasn't too worried, since, as I said, the front door was closed.

MEH IS TURNING ME INTO A **PET DETECTIVE!**

Meh is an adventurous napper. We had to look EVERY-WHERE, even in the most improbable places.

STRANGE NAP SPOTS OF THE PAST:

THE DIRTY LAUNDRY BASKET

THE RECYCLING BIN

MY
UNDERWEAR
DRAWER

THE **BOTTOM** SHELF
OF MY BOOKCASE

THE
SINK

"Well," said Chuck, "she's a real champ at hide-and-seek. You can add that to your observations."

So I did. Here goes:

OBSERVATION # 18:

OLGAMUSES ARE HIDE-AND-SEEK CHAMPIONS

"Maybe she slipped out the door when you came in?" I said. "I can't think of where to look next. It's like she vanished or evaporated."

Chuck and I stood there, not knowing what to do next, when the doorbell rang again.

It was the Lalas, all dressed up as doctors.

"Thanks for the olives," I said. "Meh seems better, but unfortunately, I have no idea where she is. I was starting to think maybe she was with you guys."

"No, she's not," they said.

"Okay, then come in. Maybe you can help me find her."

The Lalas looked a bit silly in their costumes, but I was glad they were here. I had a real search party helping me.

I'LL JUST PUT THE OLIVES IN THE FRIDGE, AND THEN WE CAN START **THE SEARCH.**

I went to the kitchen and opened the fridge door. On the bottom shelf, between a bunch of asparagus and a bowl of leftover mac and cheese, was Meh. She was surrounded by a bunch of spring rolls.

"What are you doing in the fridge, Meh?" I asked. "And where did you find those spring rolls? I don't remember buying any!"

"Olga," said Chuck, "have you ever seen spring rolls that

It was true. The spring rolls were moving. Squirming, to be more precise. And when I looked closely, I saw that they had little faces.

They were not spring rolls at all.

THEY WERE

BABiES.

BABY OLGAMUSES!!!

OH.MY.GOD.

They were so ADORABLE!

That's why Meh had been acting all weird!

She was lying on her side, looking content. She was looking at us with sleepy eyes, blinking a little bit. She was emitting a weird noise I'd never heard before that sounded like a can opener or a big electrical toothbrush.

BZZZZR
BZZRRR

She was **PURRING.**

She was **NURSING HER BABIES!**

I gently closed the fridge door to let her nurse in peace. Then Chuck and I sat down on the couch and noted down everything that had happened with Meh so far.

MAJOR SCIENTIFIC EVENT!

OBSERVATION # 19:

1. THE **PINK BUMPS** WERE NIPPLES.

DUH.

I FEEL SO **DUMB** FOR NOT HAVING THOUGHT OF THAT!

2. SO OLGAMUSES ARE IN FACT **MAMMALS!**

3. BABY OLGAMUSES, LIKE SPRING ROLLS, ARE **BEST KEPT IN THE FRIDGE.**

SPRING ROLL   BABY OLGAMUS

4. THEIR BODIES ARE **SLIGHTLY TRANSLUCENT,** LIKE . . . SPRING ROLLS.

5. THEY ARE MUCH MUCH **CUTER** THAN SPRING ROLLS, ALTHOUGH MAYBE NOT AS DELICIOUS.

PLEASE DO NOT EAT US!

Then I had a thought.

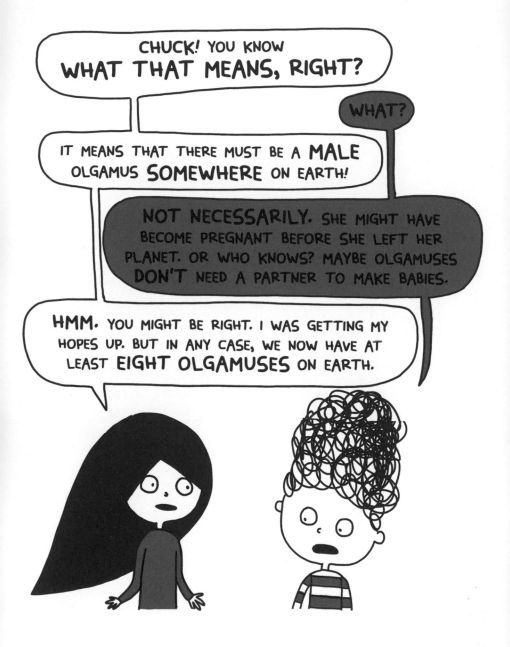

EIGHT OLGAMUSES. That's a lot more than we had
before. That meant that the Earth, and specificially my
fridge, now contained eight good reasons for me to
stay here.

These babies were not ready for a trip yet.

It was time to celebrate. Chuck and I went to Mr. Hoopah's store to get some ice cream and some fancy olives for the new mom.

Oh, and another notebook too. I'm almost out of pages in this one, and with the new babies, there will be lots of

OBSERVING TO DO.

READ BOTH!

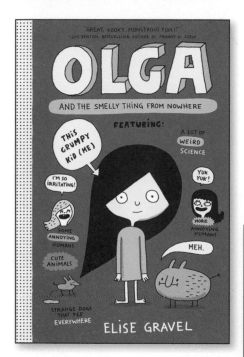

Olga's scientific adventures continue!

What else will she discover about Meh?

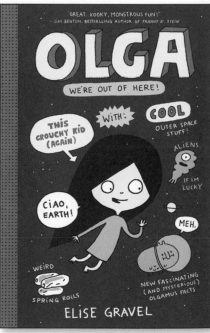